Y
Bears
Hibernation
CF

For Thomas and Max with love - *S.W.*

First published in Great Britain in 1999 by
Frances Lincoln Limited, 4 Torriano Mews
Torriano Avenue, London NW5 2RZ

British Library Cataloguing in Publication Data
available on request

ISBN 0-7112-1420-4

Set in Hiroshige Book
Printed in Hong Kong

9 8 7 6 5 4 3 2 1

Copy Me, Copycub

Richard Edwards
Illustrated by Susan Winter

FRANCES LINCOLN

It was spring in the north woods,
and the bears were out exploring.
   Everything his mother did,
the cub did too.

When his mother splashed through a swamp,
the cub splashed through a swamp.
When his mother sat down for a scratch,
the cub sat down for a scratch.

"You know what you are," said the mother bear.
"You're a little Copycub."

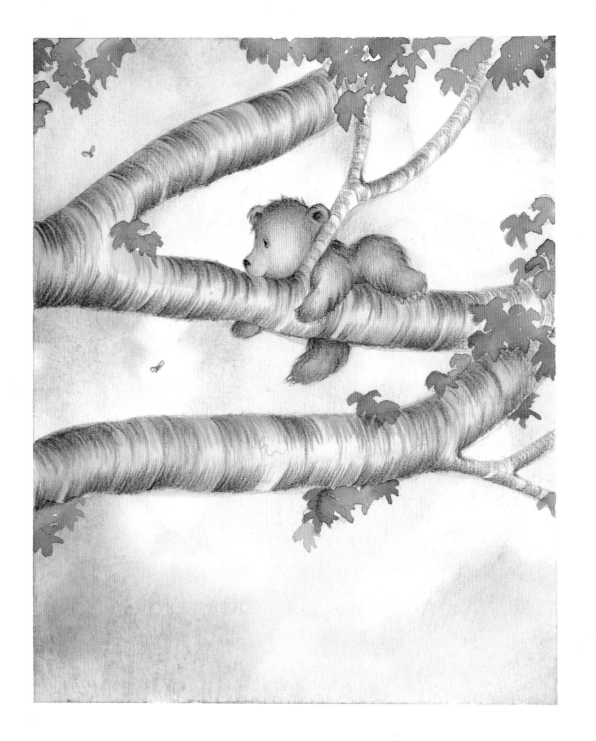

From spring into summer the bears wandered, looking for good things to eat.

When his mother picked berries, Copycub picked berries.

When his mother climbed a tree for honey, Copycub climbed a tree for honey.

"Yes, you're my own little Copycub," his mother said, giving him a hug.

Autumn came, and the days grew colder. One morning when the bears awoke, there was frost on the ground.

"It's time for us to go to our cave," said the mother bear. "Winter's coming, and soon it'll be too cold to stay outside. The bearcave will shelter us from the snow. Follow me, Copycub, and keep close behind."

His mother lolloped through the trees.
Copycub lolloped through the trees.

His mother waded streams.
Copycub waded streams.

It was a long journey for a small bear. Copycub tried his best to keep up, but he was beginning to feel very tired when something cold and wet touched the end of his nose.

It was beginning to snow.

Snow fell quickly, snow fell thickly, blowing into Copycub's eyes so he could hardly see the way. Ice fringed his fur and his paws were numb with cold. He couldn't go one step further. All he wanted to do was lie down and sleep.

But his mother came back for him.

"You can't sleep here, or you'll freeze," she said.
"Come on, Copycub, the cave's not far.
Just a few more steps. Copy me."

His mother took a step.
Copycub took a step.
His mother took another step.
Copycub took another step...
and another...
and another, until...

"We're here, Copycub!"
In a tumble of rocks was
the entrance to the bearcave.

Soon they were inside.

The cave was quiet and dry, and carpeted with leaves.

Copycub's mother hugged him until he was warm.

"We're safe now," she said. "Soon we'll be sleeping tight, and when we wake up it'll be sunny spring again."

They watched the snow falling outside. Then they snuggled down
into the leaves.

His mother yawned.
Copycub yawned.
His mother put her arms
round Copycub.
Copycub put his arms
round his mother.
His mother said,
"Good night, see you in
the springtime."
But Copycub didn't answer.

He was already asleep.